Words to Know Before

Let's Learn The **Digraph** **Wh** Sound

whacks
whale
wharf
when
where
which
whiff
whines
whistles
white
why

www.rourkeeducationalmedia.com

Edited by Precious McKenzie
Illustrated by Ed Myer
Art Direction, Cover and Page Layout by Tara Raymo

Library of Congress PCN Data

Watch for Whales! / Meg Greve
ISBN 978-1-62169-269-0 (hard cover) (alk. paper)
ISBN 978-1-62169-227-0 (soft cover)
Library of Congress Control Number: 2012952774

Rourke Educational Media
Printed in the United States of America,
North Mankato, Minnesota

rourkeeducationalmedia.com

customerservice@rourkeeducationalmedia.com • PO Box 643328 Vero Beach, Florida 32964

WATCH FOR WHALES!

Counselor
Gus

Counselor
Mindy

Captain

Fitz

Dex

Lizzie

Ana

Written By Meg Greve
Illustrated By Ed Myer

"Let's go on an adventure!" says Counselor Gus.

"Where are we going?" asks Lizzie.

"When are we going?" asks Dex.

"Why are we going?" whines Fitz.

CAMP ADVENTURE

"We are going whale watching at the wharf!" says Counselor Mindy.

"What's a wharf?" asks Ana.

"It's a place where ships can stop," says Counselor Gus.

"And we get on!" says Counselor Mindy.

"Whoopee!" shout the campers.

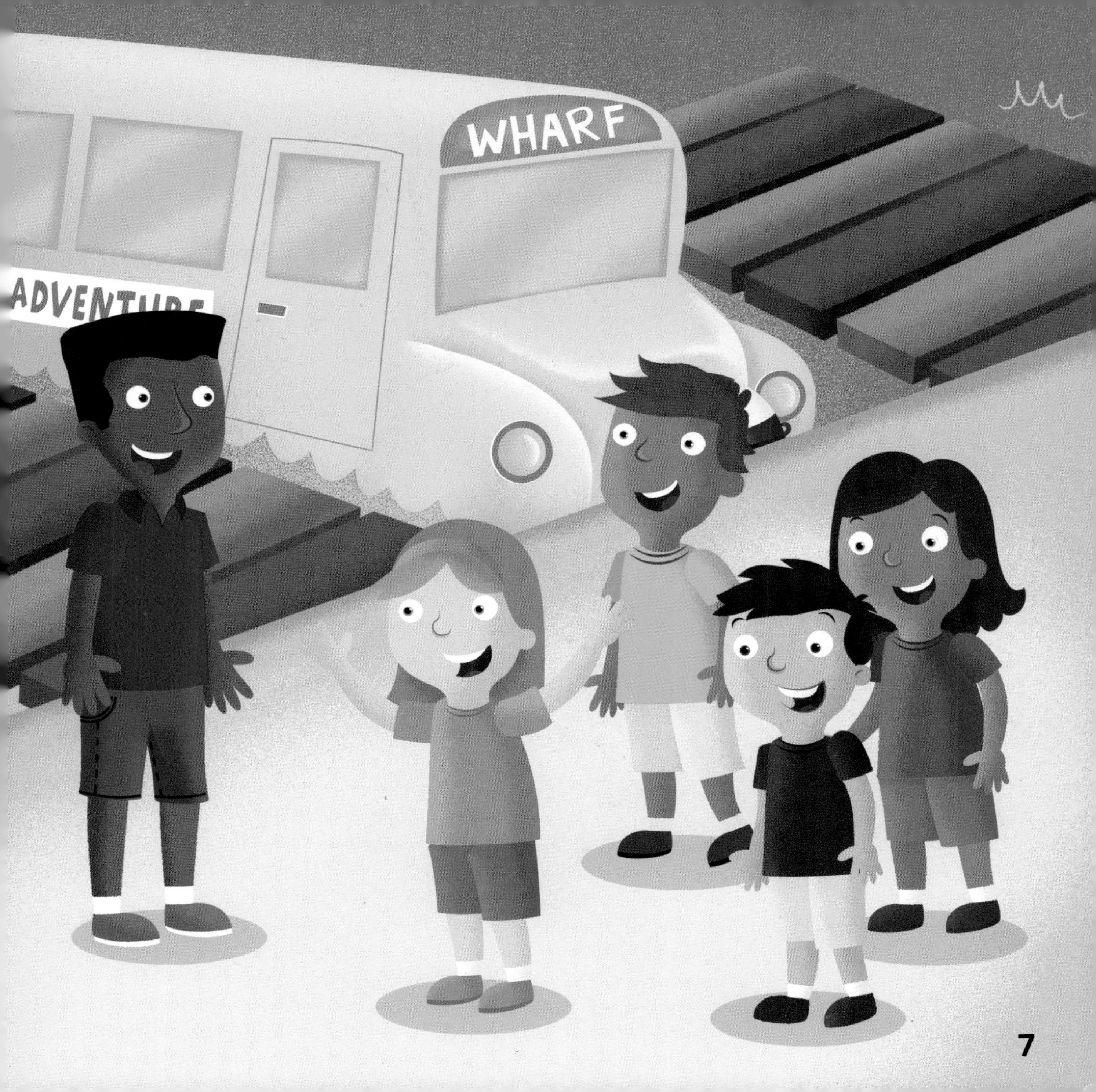
WHARF
ADVENTURE

"Whew! We're here," says Counselor Gus.

"Eeww, I got a whiff of fish," says Ana.

The campers find the great whale watching ship.

The captain whistles to the campers and says, "All aboard! Which one of you wants to see a whale?"

All the campers shout, "Me! Me!"

A storm springs
up at sea.

"Bad news campers! I can't see
anything. We are lost!" shouts
the captain.

"What will we do?" wail the campers.

"Where are the whales?" asks Dex.

A big white tail whacks the water.

Whap! Whap!

Water whooshes up and the campers cheer.

"Follow that whale!" shouts Lizzie.

The ship follows the whale across the white capped water.

The campers see the wharf.

"The white whale saved us!" shout the campers.

After Reading Word Study

Picture Glossary

Directions: Look at each picture and read the definition. Write a list of all of the words you know that start with the same sound as *whale*. Remember to look in the book for more words.

whacks (WAX): Whacks is a slang word. It means to hit.

whale (WAYL): A whale is a large mammal that lives in the sea.

wharf (WARF): A wharf is a place where ships can dock.

whiff (WIFF): A whiff is a quick, faint odor.

whines (WINEZ): When someone whines that means they complain or cry.

white (WITE): White is a light shade, like the color of milk.

About the Author

Meg Greve lives in Chicago with her husband and her two kids named Madison and William. She went whale watching and saw humpback whales with their babies!

Ask The Author!
www.rem4students.com

About the Illustrator

Ed Myer is a Manchester-born illustrator now living in London. After growing up in an artistic household, Ed studied ceramics at university but always continued drawing pictures. As well as illustration, Ed likes traveling, playing computer games, and walking little Ted (his Jack Russell).